Bravo Phonics

Cecilia Chan

U0064141

Level 2

The Commercial Press

Edited by: Betty Wong

Cover designed by: Cathy Chiu

Typeset by: Summer Xiao

Printing arranged by: Kenneth Lung

Bravo Phonics (Level 2)

Author:	Cecilia Chan
Publisher:	The Commercial Press (H.K.) Ltd.
	8/F, Eastern Central Plaza, 3 Yiu Hing Road, Shau Kei Wan, H.K.
	http://www.commercialpress.com.hk
Distributor:	THE SUP Publishing Logistics (H.K.) Ltd.
	16/F, Tsuen Wan Industrial Building, 220-248 Texaco Road,
	Tsuen Wan, NT, Hong Kong
Printer:	Elegance Printing and Book Binding Co., Ltd.
	Block A, 4/F, Hoi Bun Industrial Building 6 Wing Yip Street,
	Kwun Tung Kowloon, Hong Kong

© 2023 The Commercial Press (H.K.) Ltd.

First edition, First printing, July 2023

ISBN 978 962 07 0621 9

Printed in Hong Kong

Bravo Phonics Series is a special gift to all children – the ability to READ ENGLISH accurately and fluently!

ENJOY!

About the Author

The author, Ms Cecilia Chan, is a well-known English educator with many years of teaching experience. Passionate and experienced in teaching English, Ms Chan has taught students from over 30 schools in Hong Kong, including Marymount Primary School, Marymount Secondary School, Diocesan Boys' School, Diocesan Girls' School, St. Paul's Co-educational College, St. Paul's Co-educational College Primary School, St. Paul's College, St. Paul's Convent School (Primary and Secondary Sections), Belilios Public School, Raimondi College Primary Section, St. Clare's Primary School, St. Joseph's Primary School, St. Joseph's College, Pun U Association Wah Yan Primary School and other international schools. Many of Ms Chan's students have won prizes in Solo Verse Speaking, Prose Reading and Public Speaking at the Hong Kong Schools Speech Festival and

other interschool open speech contests. Driven by her passion in promoting English learning, Ms Chan has launched the Bravo Phonics Series (Levels 1-5) as an effective tool to foster a love of English reading and learning in children.

To all my Beloved Students

Acknowledgement

Many thanks to the Editor, JY Ho, for her effort and contribution to the editing of the Bravo Phonics Series and her assistance all along.

Author's Words

The fundamental objective of phonics teaching is to develop step-by-step a child's ability to pronounce and recognize the words in the English language. Each phonic activity is a means to build up the child's power of word recognition until such power has been thoroughly exercised that word recognition becomes practically automatic.

Proper phonic training is highly important to young children especially those with English as a second language. It enables a child to acquire a large reading vocabulary in a comparatively short time and hence can happily enjoy fluent story reading. By giving phonics a place in the daily allotment of children's activities, they can be brought to a state of reading proficiency at an early age. Be patient, allow ample time for children to enjoy each and every phonic activity; if it is well and truly done, further steps will be taken easily and much more quickly.

Bravo Phonics Series has proven to be of value in helping young children reach the above objective and embark joyfully on the voyage of learning to read. It consists of five books of five levels, covering all the letter sounds of the consonants, short and long vowels, diphthongs and blends in the English language. Bravo Phonics Series employs a step-by-step approach, integrating different learning skills through a variety of fun reading, writing, drawing, spelling and story-telling activities. There are quizzes, drills, tongue twisters, riddles and comprehension exercises to help consolidate all the letter sounds learnt. The QR code on each page enables a child to self-learn at home by following the instructions of Ms Chan while simultaneously practising the letter sounds through the example given.

The reward to teachers and parents will be a thousandfold when children gain self-confidence and begin to apply their phonic experiences to happy story reading.

Contents

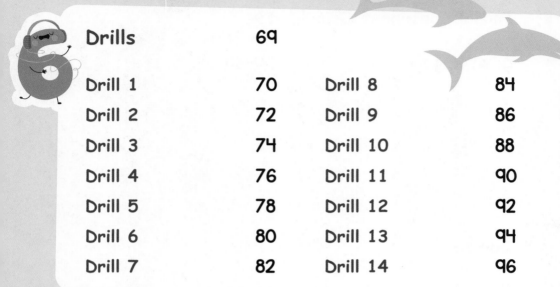

Quick Guide

 Say   Circle   Write   Scan

 Colour  Read Draw

Hello, this is Ms Chan. How are you?
Are you ready to learn Bravo Phonics?
Let's learn about Consonant Sounds!

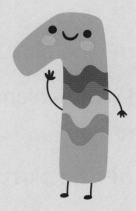

Initial Consonant Sounds

s
p
f
m
h
n
t
r

Initial Consonant Sounds

 Say the names of the pictures.

 Write the sound with which each picture begins on the line.

 Say the names of the pictures after me.

t
_____

_____

_____

2

_____

_____

_____

_____

 Now colour the pictures.

Initial Consonant Sounds

 Say the names of the pictures.

 Write the sound with which each picture begins on the line.

 Say the names of the pictures after me.

f

4

_____

_____

_____

 Now colour the pictures.

Initial Consonant Sounds

SCAN ME

 Say the names of the pictures.

 Write the sound with which each picture begins on the line.

 Say the names of the pictures after me.

m _____

_____

_____

6

_____

_____

_____

_____

 Now colour the pictures.

7

Initial Consonant Sounds

 Say the names of the pictures.

 Write the sound with which each pictures begins on the line.

 Say the names of the pictures after me.

b

_____

_____

_____

_____

 Now colour the pictures.

q

Let's learn more
Consonant Sounds!

Final Consonant Sounds

p

n

t

m

Final Consonant Sounds

Say the names of the pictures.

Write the sound with which each picture ends on the line.

Say the names of the pictures after me.

n

_____

_____

 Now colour the pictures.

Final Consonant Sounds

Say the names of the pictures.

Write the sound with which each picture ends on the line.

Say the names of the pictures after me.

p

_____

_____

_____

_____

_____

_____

 Now colour the pictures.

15

Say the words in each box from left to right.

 Circle those words that end with the same sound.

 man  ham fan tap can

| sit | fit | ran | top | lit |

cat	rat	cot	fat	map

fin	ham	ram	lip	sam

top	mop	lot	hop	sum

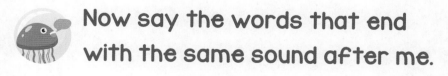 Now say the words that end with the same sound after me.

17

Final Consonant Sounds

 Say the words in each box from left to right.

 Circle those words that end with the same sound.

cap   (tan)   (ran)   (ban)   fat

sip   lip   pin   hot   tip

| lap | ant | map | cap | fin |

| hot | lap | rot | dot | ten |

| hop | dim | sim | pan | him |

 Now say the words that end with the same sound after me.

Say the first sound.

 Circle one of the other sounds to build the word that matches the picture.

 Write the word on the line.

fa (t (n) r)   to (p n m)

fan _____   _____

pi (m p n)   an (r t n)

ha (n m p)   do (r t n)

 Say the names of the pictures after me.

 Now colour the pictures.

Say the first sound.

 Circle one of the other sounds to build the word that matches the picture.

 Write the word on the line.

dru (n (m) p)   lam (b p r)

drum

ten (t p m)   lio (p m n)

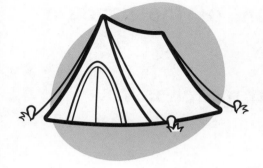 

rai (m p n)   swi (n t m)

 Say the names of the pictures after me.

 Now colour the pictures.

Final Consonant Sounds

 Say the words in each box after me.

 Draw a picture of one of the words in each group.

 Circle the word that matches your picture.

 Write the word on the line.

 Colour your pictures.

bat

cat

hat

man
fan
can

hot
dot
pot

Final Consonant Sounds

 Say the words in each box after me.

 Draw a picture of one of the words in each group.

 Circle the word that matches your picture.

 Write the word on the line.

 Colour your pictures.

| hop |
| top |
| mop |

bin

pin

fin

ham

jam

sam

Let's learn more
Consonant Sounds!

Initial Consonant Sounds

g

w

k

j

g

SCAN ME

Say the names of the pictures.

Write the sound with which each picture begins on the line.

Say the names of the pictures after me.

g

Write the sound 'g'.

 Say it aloud as you write it.

G g G g G g

 Now colour the pictures.

g

Say the names of the pictures.

Circle those pictures that begin with the sound 'g'.

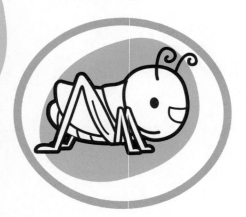

g

32

g

 Say the names of the pictures with the sound 'g' after me.

 Now colour the pictures that begin with the sound 'g'.

Say the names of the pictures.

Write the sound with which each picture begins on the line.

Say the names of the pictures after me.

W

Write the sound 'w'.

 Say it aloud as you write it.

W w W w

 Now colour the pictures.

35

Say the names of the pictures.

Circle those pictures that begin with the sound 'w'.

36

 Say the names of the pictures with the sound 'w' after me.

 Now colour the pictures that begin with the sound 'w'.

Say the names of the pictures.

Write the sound with which each picture begins on the line.

Say the names of the pictures after me.

k

Write the sound 'k'.

 Say it aloud as you write it.

Kk Kk Kk

 Now colour the pictures.

39

Say the names of the pictures.

Circle those pictures that begin with the sound 'k'.

k

 Say the names of the pictures that begin with the sound 'k' after me.

 Now colour the pictures that begin with the sound 'k'.

41

j

Say the names of the pictures.

Write the sound with which each picture begins on the line.

Say the names of the pictures after me.

j

_____

_____

_____

_____

_____

Write the sound 'j'.

 Say it aloud as you write it.

J j J j J j J j

 Now colour the pictures.

43

j

Say the names of the pictures.

Circle those pictures that begin with the sound 'j'.

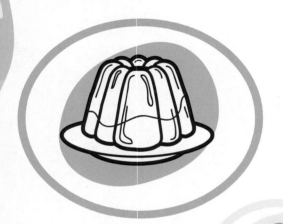

j

 Say the names of the pictures with the sound 'j' after me.

 Now colour the pictures that begin with the sound 'j'.

Are you ready for the Quizzes?
Let's start!

Quizzes

Say the names of the pictures.

Circle the correct sound with which each picture begins.

g w k j   **k g j w**   **j w g k**

w j g k   **k g j w**   **j w g k**

Now say the names of the pictures after me.

Score

/6

48

Quiz 4.2

 Say the names of the pictures.

 Circle the correct sound with which each picture begins.

g k w j

w j k g

g w j k

w j g k

k g w j

k g w j

 Now say the names of the pictures after me.

Score /6

49

Quiz 4.3

SCAN ME

Say the names of the pictures.

Write the sound with which each picture begins on the line.

_____ _____ _____

_____ _____ _____

Now say the names of the pictures after me.

Score

/6

50

Quiz 4.4

Say the names of the pictures.

Write the sound with which each picture begins on the line.

_____   _____   _____

_____   _____   _____

Now say the names of the pictures after me.

Score

/6

51

Say the names of the pictures.

 Circle the word that matches each picture.

king
wing
sing

bar
jar
far

good
hood
wood

ham
jam
ram

match
catch
watch

late
gate
rate

 Now say the names of the pictures after me.

Score
/6

Quiz 4.6

 Say the names of the pictures.

 Circle the word that matches each picture.

wing
ring
ding

kiss
miss
hiss

saw
raw
jaw

moose
goose
loose

brass
grass
mass

white
kite
bite

 Now say the names of the pictures after me.

Score

/6

53

Say the names of the pictures.

Spell the name of each picture by writing the sound with which the picture begins.

_____ ing

_____ ig

_____ un

_____ ey

_____ itchen

_____ ar

Now spell and say the names of the pictures after me.

Score

/6

54

Say the names of the pictures.

 Spell the name of each picture by writing the sound with which the picture begins.

_____ ump

_____ ood

_____ ite

_____ ater

_____ oat

_____ loves

 Now spell and say the names of the pictures after me.

Score

/6

55

Say the names of the pictures.

Spell the name of each picture by writing the sound with which the picture begins.

_____ iss   _____ indow   _____ rass

_____ elly   _____ uitar   _____ ind

Now spell and say the names of the pictures after me.

Score

/6

56

Quiz 4.10

 Say the names of the pictures.

 Spell the name of each pictures by writing the sound with which the picture begins.

_____ oose

_____ all

_____ eans

_____ atch

_____ ick

_____ itten

 Now spell and say the names of the pictures after me.

Score

/6

57

Let's learn about Vowel Sounds!

3

Vowel Sounds

Short 'u'

Short 'e'

Say the names of the pictures.

Write the sound with which each picture begins on the line.

Say the names of the pictures after me.

u _____

_____

_____

_____

60

Write the sound 'u'.

 Say it aloud as you write it.

U u U u U u

 Now colour the pictures.

u

Say the names of the pictures.

Circle those pictures that begin with the sound 'u'.

u

u

 Say the names of the pictures with the sound 'u' after me.

 Now colour the pictures that begin with the sound 'u'.

Say the names of the pictures.

Write the sound with which each picture begins on the line.

Say the names of the pictures after me.

e
_____

_____

_____

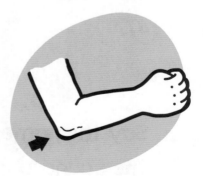

_____

Write the sound 'e'.

 Say it aloud as you write it.

E e E e E e

 Now colour the pictures.

Say the names of the pictures.

Circle those pictures that begin with the sound 'e'.

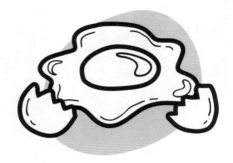

e

 Say the names of the pictures with the sound 'e' after me.

 Now colour the pictures that begin with the sound 'e'.

Are you ready for more practice? Let's begin!

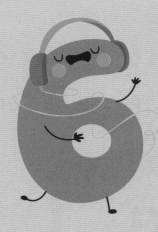

Drills

Say each sound along the line.

 Circle those that have the same sound as the first one.

g (g) (g) j k (g)

w w j w k w

k k k g j k

j j g j w j

w   k   w   j   w   w

k   g   k   k   j   k

j   w   j   j   g   j

g   j   g   k   g   g

 Now say the sounds after me.

Say each sound along the line.

 Circle those that have the same sound as the first one.

a a e a o a

e e e i a e e

i a i i u i

o u o o o a

u e u o u u

 Now say the sounds after me.

73

Say the sounds in each box.

Write the two letters together to form a new sound.

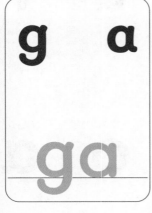

g a

ga

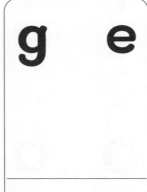

g e

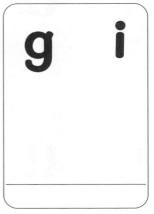

g i

g o

g u

k a k e k i

k o k u

 Now say the sounds after me.

Say the sounds in each box.

Write the two letters together to form a new sound.

w a

wa

w e

w i

w o

w u

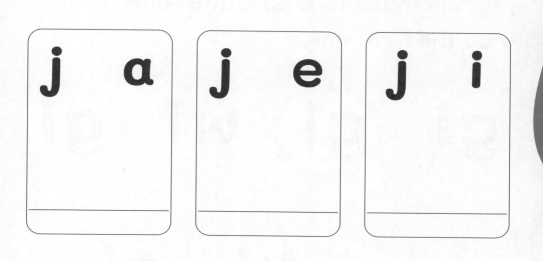

ja je ji

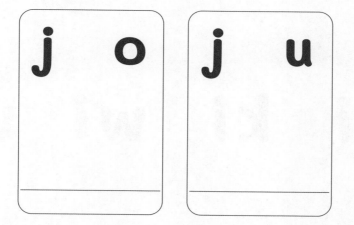

jo ju

 Now say the sounds after me.

Say each sound along the line.

Circle those that have the same sound as the first one.

gi (gi) wi (gi)

ki (gi)

wi ki wi wi

wi gi

ki gi ki ki

ji ki

ji ji ji ki

gi ji

 Now say the sounds after me.

Say each sound along the line.

Circle those that have the same sound as the first one.

ge   ge   ge   ke

ge   we

we   we   je   we

ke   we

ke je ke ge

ke ke

ji ge je we

je je

 Now say the sounds after me.

Say each sound along the line.

Circle those that have the same sound as the first one.

sa (**sa**) **wa** (**sa**)

ka (**sa**)

ra **ka** **ra** **ra**

ra **ga**

ca ga ca ca

ja ca

pa pa pa ka

ga pa

 Now say the sounds after me.

Say each sound along the line.

 Circle those that have the same sound as the first one.

no (no) wo (no)

ko (no)

fo ko fo fo

fo go

lo go lo lo

jo lo

bo bo bo ko

go bo

 Now say the sounds after me.

Say each sound along the line.

Circle those that have the same sound as the first one.

tu (tu) wu (tu)

ku (tu)

hu ku hu hu

hu gu

du gu du du

ju du

mu mu mu ku

gu mu

 Now say the sounds after me.

Say the sounds in each box.

Write the two sounds together to form a word.

ma **ss**	**ba** **ss**
mass	

we	ll	be	ll

bu	ff	cu	ff

 Now say the sounds after me.

Say the sounds in each box.

Write the two sounds together to form a word.

mo	ss

moss

bo	ss

ti ll	si ll
tu ff	mu ff

 Now say the sounds after me.

Say the sounds in each box.

Write the two sounds together to form a word.

to **ss**	**lo** **ss**
toss	

ki   ll

mi   ll

pu   ff

ru   ff

 Now say the sounds after me.

q3

SCAN ME

Say the words in each box.

Circle those words that rhyme with the first one.

mass **bass**

tell puff **lass**

tell   sell

bell well puff

puff   loss

bass muff ruff

 Now say the words that rhyme after me.

Say the words in each box.

 Circle those words that rhyme with the first one.

loss   **(moss)**

buff **(toss)** **(cross)**

will   gill

kill   mill   well

guff   mass

tuff   bell   cuff

 Now say the words that rhyme after me.

Let's learn more Consonant Sounds!

Final Consonant Sounds

b	l	m
d	p	ss
g	n	ll
k	t	ff

Final Consonant Sounds

 Say the names of the pictures.

 Write the sound with which each picture ends on the line.

d _____   _____

_____   _____   _____

 Say the names of the pictures after me.

 Now colour the pictures.

 100

Say the names of the pictures.

 Write the sound with which each picture ends on the line.

k

_____   _____

_____   _____

 Say the names of the pictures after me.

 Now colour the pictures.

101

Final Consonant Sounds

 Say the names of the pictures.

 Write the sound with which each picture ends on the line.

p _____   _____

_____   _____

 Say the names of the pictures after me.

 Now colour the pictures.

102

Say the names of the pictures.

 Write the sound with which each picture ends on the line.

n
_____   _____

_____

 Say the names of the pictures after me.

 Now colour the pictures.

Final Consonant Sounds

Say the first sound.

Circle one of the other sounds to build the word that matches the picture.

Write the word on the line.

be (k b **d**)   ba (g l d)

bed

_____

des (b l **k**)   bow (k l **t**)

_____   _____

for (**t** k l)

_____

 Say the names of the pictures after me.

 Now colour the pictures.

Say the first sound.

 Circle one of the other sounds to build the word that matches the picture.

 Write the word on the line.

hee (n **l** p)   ma (p t k)

heel

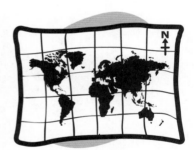

106

moo (m n l) ju (g k m)

_____   _____

kic (k t l)

_____

 Say the names of the pictures after me.

 Now colour the pictures.

Say the first sound.

 Circle one of the other sounds to build the word that matches the picture.

 Write the word on the line.

ho (p **t** n)   su (m n p)

hot
_____   _____

ca (**t** p d) gir (l **m** n)

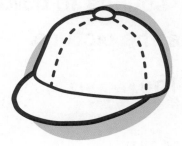 

_____

dru (**n** m l)

_____

 Say the names of the pictures after me.

 Now colour the pictures.

Final Consonant Sounds

 Say the first sound.

 Circle one of the other sounds to build the word that matches the picture.

 Write the word on the line.

) bi (ff ss (ll))   be (ff   ll   ss)

bill

_____

ki (ll ff ss)   pu (ss ll ff)

_____   _____

we (ff ss ll)

_____

 Say the names of the pictures after me.

 Now colour the pictures.

Say the words in each box after me.

 Draw a picture of one of the words in each group.

 Circle the word that matches your picture.

 Write the word on the line.

 Colour your pictures.

ball

wall

fall

hen
ten
pen

kite
write
bite

Say the words in each box after me.

 Draw a picture of one of the words in each group.

 Circle the word that matches your picture.

 Write the word on the line.

 Colour your pictures.

| wing |
| ring |
| sing |

mug
rug
hug

drum
plum
sum

Are you ready for the challenge?
Let's begin!

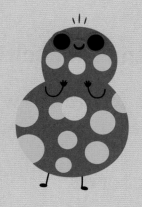

Read and Draw

Read the sentence in each box after me.

Draw a picture to match what you read in each box.

Colour your pictures.

I can sing.

I can run.

Read the sentence in each box after me.

Draw a picture to match what you read in each box.

Colour your pictures.

I kiss Mom.

I play with Dad.

Read the words in each box after me.

 Draw a picture to match what you read in each box.

 Colour your pictures.

A man with a gun.

A doll in a bed.

Read and Draw

 Read the words in each box after me.

 Draw what the words tell you to do.

 Colour your pictures.

Draw a hat on the girl.

Draw a bell on the dog.

Read the words in each box after me.

 Draw what the words tell you to do.

 Colour your pictures.

Draw six stars in the sky.

Draw eight eggs on
the plate.

Read and Draw

 Read the words in each box after me.

 Draw what the words tell you to do.

 Colour your pictures.

Draw a lid on the pot.

Draw five candles on the cake.

129

Are you ready for the challenge? Let's begin!

Say and Match

Say the words in the box after me.

Find the words that match each picture and write them on the line.

A lion   **A snake**

A hen   **A monkey**

_____

_____

_____

_____

 Say the words after me.

 Now colour the pictures.

Say and Match

Say the words in the box after me.

Find the words that match each picture and write them on the line.

A bell	**A drum**
A desk	**A lamp**

_____

_____

_____

 Say the words after me.

 Now colour the pictures.

Say and Match

 Say the words in the box after me.

 Find the words that match each picture and write them on the line.

Run	**Sit**
Stand	**Hop**

_____

_____

_____

_____

 Say the words after me.

 Now colour the pictures.

137

Say the words in the box after me.

Find the words that match each picture and write them on the line.

Cry	**Smile**
Laugh	**Sleep**

_____

_____

_____

_____

 Say the words after me.

 Now colour the pictures.

Are you ready for the challenge?
They are great fun!

Tell a Story

SCAN ME

Read the sentence in each box after me.

Draw a picture to match the sentence in each box.
The pictures tell a story.

Colour your pictures.

1

I eat the bread.

2

I drink the milk.

3

I go to school.

Well done, students! You can check your answers with the Answer Key.

Answer Key

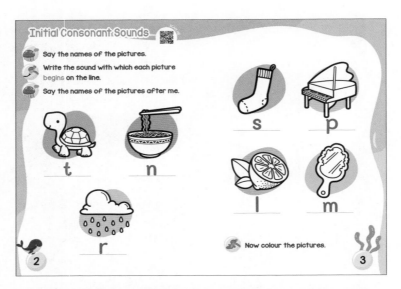

Initial Consonant Sounds

- Say the names of the pictures.
- Write the sound with which each picture begins on the line.
- Say the names of the pictures after me.

t

n

r

s

p

l

m

Now colour the pictures.

2

3

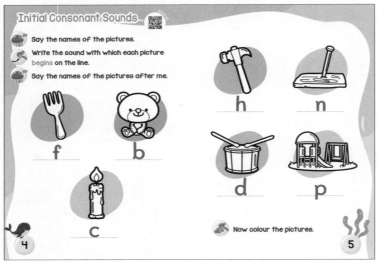

Initial Consonant Sounds

- Say the names of the pictures.
- Write the sound with which each picture begins on the line.
- Say the names of the pictures after me.

f

b

c

h

n

d

p

Now colour the pictures.

4

5

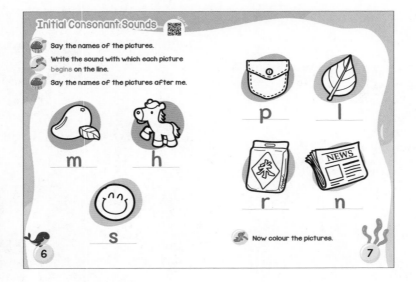

Initial Consonant Sounds

- Say the names of the pictures.
- Write the sound with which each picture begins on the line.
- Say the names of the pictures after me.

m

h

s

p

l

r

n

Now colour the pictures.

6

7

146

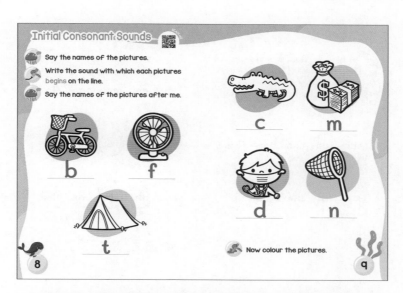

Initial Consonant Sounds

- Say the names of the pictures.
- Write the sound with which each pictures **begins** on the line.
- Say the names of the pictures after me.

b

f

t

c

m

d

n

Now colour the pictures.

8

9

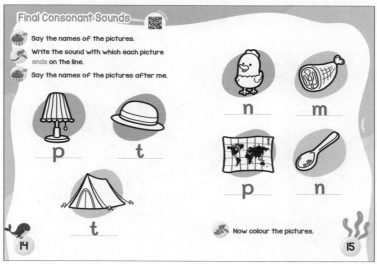

Final Consonant Sounds

- Say the names of the pictures.
- Write the sound with which each picture **ends** on the line.
- Say the names of the pictures after me.

p

t

t

n

m

p

n

Now colour the pictures.

14

15

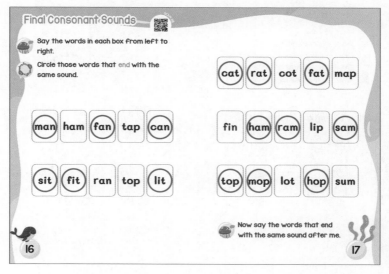

Final Consonant Sounds

- Say the words in each box from left to right.
- Circle those words that **end** with the same sound.

(cat) (rat) cot (fat) map

(man) ham (fan) tap (can)

fin (ham) (ram) lip (sam)

(sit) (fit) ran top (lit)

(top) (mop) lot (hop) sum

Now say the words that end with the same sound after me.

16

17

147

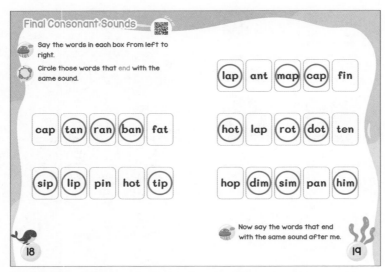

Final Consonant Sounds

Say the words in each box from left to right.

Circle those words that end with the same sound.

(lap) ant (map) (cap) fin

cap (tan) (ran) (ban) fat

(hot) lap (rot) (dot) ten

(sip) (lip) pin hot (tip)

hop (dim) (sim) pan (him)

Now say the words that end with the same sound after me.

18   19

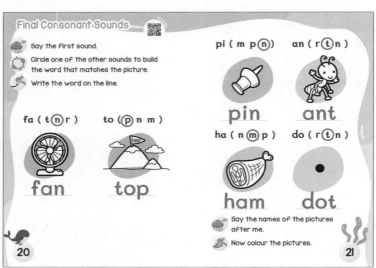

Final Consonant Sounds

Say the first sound.

Circle one of the other sounds to build the word that matches the picture.

Write the word on the line.

pi (m p (n))   an (r (t) n)

pin   ant

fa (t (n) r)   to ((p) n m)

ha (n (m) p)   do (r (t) n)

fan   top

ham   dot

Say the names of the pictures after me.

Now colour the pictures.

20   21

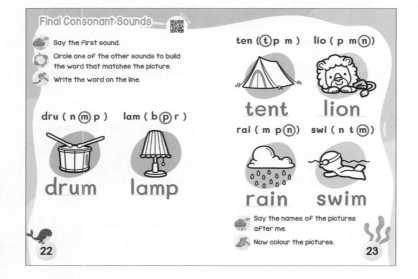

Final Consonant Sounds

Say the first sound.

Circle one of the other sounds to build the word that matches the picture.

Write the word on the line.

ten ((t) p m)   lio (p m (n))

tent   lion

dru (n (m) p)   lam (b (p) r)

rai (m p (n))   swi (n t (m))

drum   lamp

rain   swim

Say the names of the pictures after me.

Now colour the pictures.

148   22   23

Final Consonant Sounds

- Say the words in each box after me.
- Draw a picture of one of the words in each group.
- Circle the word that matches your picture.
- Write the word on the line.
- Colour your pictures.

man
fan
can

man *Suggested Answer*

bat
cat
hat

cat *Suggested Answer*

hot
dot
pot

dot *Suggested Answer*

24

25

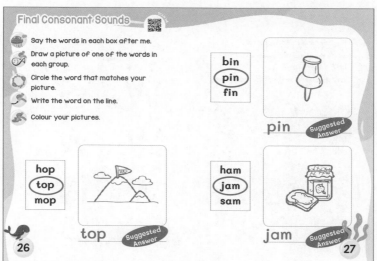

Final Consonant Sounds

- Say the words in each box after me.
- Draw a picture of one of the words in each group.
- Circle the word that matches your picture.
- Write the word on the line.
- Colour your pictures.

bin
pin
fin

pin *Suggested Answer*

hop
top
mop

top *Suggested Answer*

ham
jam
sam

jam *Suggested Answer*

26

27

g

- Say the names of the pictures.
- Write the sound with which each picture begins on the line.
- Say the names of the pictures after me.

- Write the sound 'g'.
- Say it aloud as you write it.

g

g

g

g

g

g

G g G g G g

G g G g G g

G g G g G g

- Now colour the pictures.

30

31

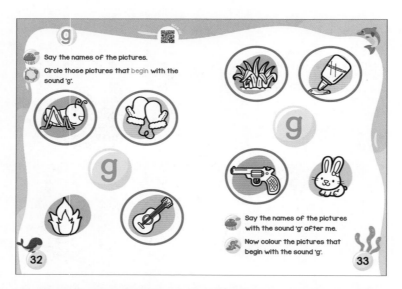

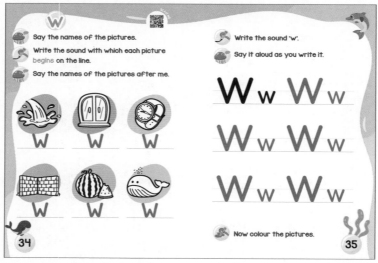

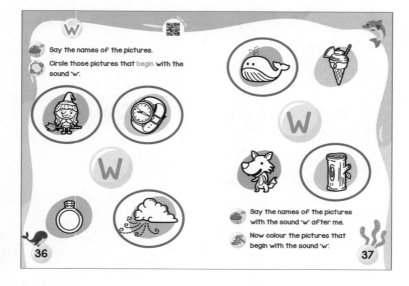

Say the names of the pictures.

Write the sound with which each picture begins on the line.

Say the names of the pictures after me.

k   k   k

k   k   k

Write the sound 'k'.

Say it aloud as you write it.

Kk Kk Kk

Kk Kk Kk

Kk Kk Kk

Now colour the pictures.

38   39

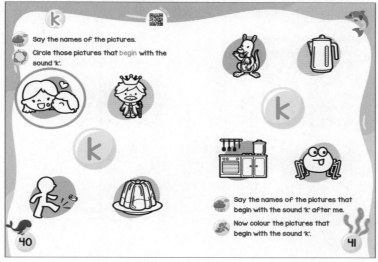

Say the names of the pictures.

Circle those pictures that begin with the sound 'k'.

k

Say the names of the pictures that begin with the sound 'k' after me.

Now colour the pictures that begin with the sound 'k'.

40   41

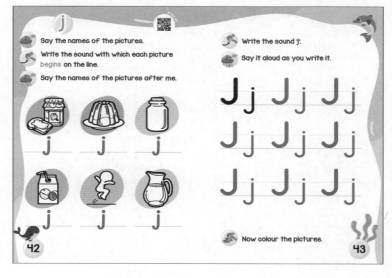

Say the names of the pictures.

Write the sound with which each picture begins on the line.

Say the names of the pictures after me.

j   j   j

j   j   j

Write the sound 'j'.

Say it aloud as you write it.

Jj Jj Jj

Jj Jj Jj

Jj Jj Jj

Now colour the pictures.

42   43

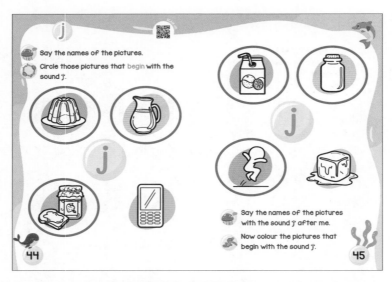

j

Say the names of the pictures.

Circle those pictures that begin with the sound *j*.

j

j

Say the names of the pictures with the sound *j* after me.

Now colour the pictures that begin with the sound *j*.

44

45

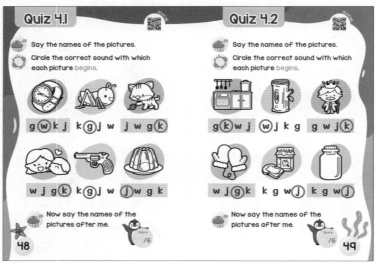

Quiz 4.1

Say the names of the pictures.

Circle the correct sound with which each picture begins.

g w k j   k g j w   j w g k

w j g k   k g j w   j w g k

Now say the names of the pictures after me.

Score /6

48

Quiz 4.2

Say the names of the pictures.

Circle the correct sound with which each picture begins.

g k w j   w j k g   g w j k

w j g k   k g w j   k g w j

Now say the names of the pictures after me.

Score /6

49

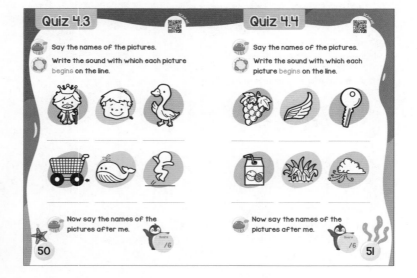

Quiz 4.3

Say the names of the pictures.

Write the sound with which each picture begins on the line.

_____   _____   _____

_____   _____   _____

Now say the names of the pictures after me.

Score /6

50

Quiz 4.4

Say the names of the pictures.

Write the sound with which each picture begins on the line.

_____   _____   _____

_____   _____   _____

Now say the names of the pictures after me.

Score /6

51

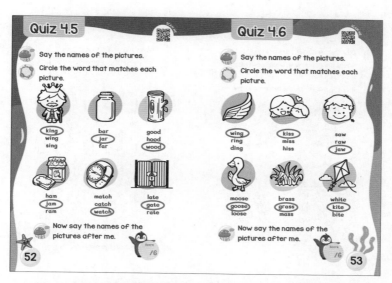

Quiz 4.5

Say the names of the pictures.

Circle the word that matches each picture.

king
(wing)
sing

bar
(jar)
far

good
hood
(wood)

ham
(jam)
ram

match
catch
(watch)

late
gate
rate

Now say the names of the pictures after me.

52

Score /6

Quiz 4.6

Say the names of the pictures.

Circle the word that matches each picture.

(wing)
ring
ding

(kiss)
miss
hiss

saw
raw
(jaw)

moose
(goose)
loose

brass
(grass)
mass

white
(kite)
bite

Now say the names of the pictures after me.

Score /6

53

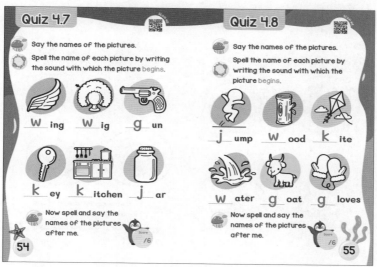

Quiz 4.7

Say the names of the pictures.

Spell the name of each picture by writing the sound with which the picture begins.

W ing   W ig   g un

k ey   k itchen   j ar

Now spell and say the names of the pictures after me.

54

Score /6

Quiz 4.8

Say the names of the pictures.

Spell the name of each picture by writing the sound with which the picture begins.

j ump   W ood   k ite

W ater   g oat   g loves

Now spell and say the names of the pictures after me.

Score /6

55

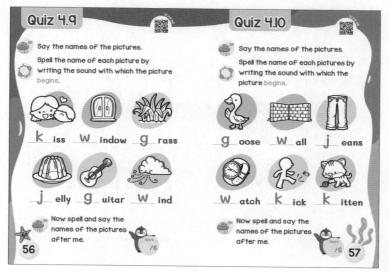

Quiz 4.9

Say the names of the pictures.

Spell the name of each picture by writing the sound with which the picture begins.

k iss   W indow   g rass

j elly   g uitar   W ind

Now spell and say the names of the pictures after me.

56

Score /6

Quiz 4.10

Say the names of the pictures.

Spell the name of each pictures by writing the sound with which the picture begins.

g oose   W all   j eans

W atch   k ick   k itten

Now spell and say the names of the pictures after me.

Score /6   57

153

Say the names of the pictures.

Write the sound with which each picture begins on the line.

Say the names of the pictures after me.

u

u

u

u

Write the sound 'u'.

Say it aloud as you write it.

Uu Uu Uu

Uu Uu Uu

Uu Uu Uu

Now colour the pictures.

60

61

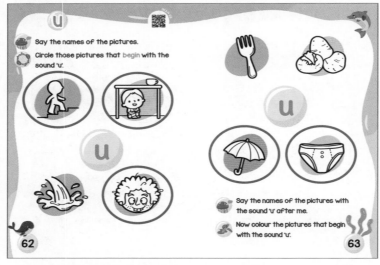

Say the names of the pictures.

Circle those pictures that begin with the sound 'u'.

u

u

Say the names of the pictures with the sound 'u' after me.

Now colour the pictures that begin with the sound 'u'.

62

63

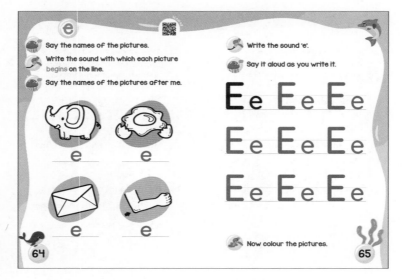

Say the names of the pictures.

Write the sound with which each picture begins on the line.

Say the names of the pictures after me.

e

e

e

e

Write the sound 'e'.

Say it aloud as you write it.

Ee Ee Ee

Ee Ee Ee

Ee Ee Ee

Now colour the pictures.

64

65

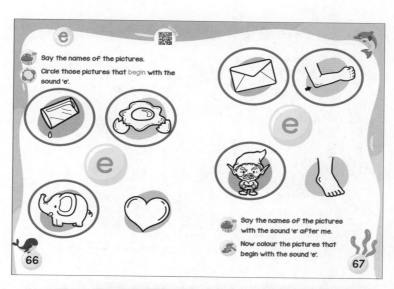

Say the names of the pictures.

Circle those pictures that begin with the sound 'e'.

Say the names of the pictures with the sound 'e' after me.

Now colour the pictures that begin with the sound 'e'.

66

67

Drill 6.1

Say each sound along the line.

Circle those that have the same sound as the first one.

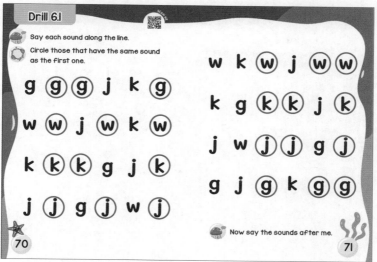

Now say the sounds after me.

70

71

Drill 6.2

Say each sound along the line.

Circle those that have the same sound as the first one.

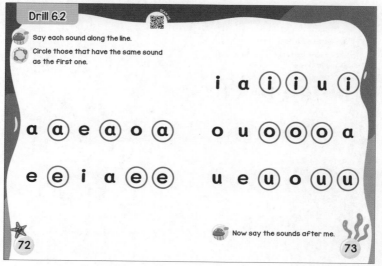

Now say the sounds after me.

72

73

155

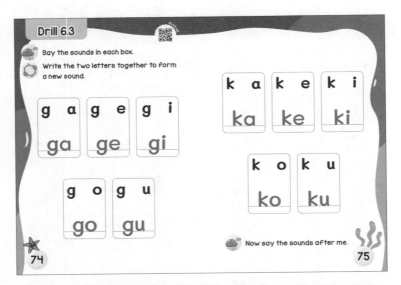

Drill 6.3

Say the sounds in each box.

Write the two letters together to form a new sound.

g	a
ga	

g	e
ge	

g	i
gi	

g	o
go	

g	u
gu	

k	a
ka	

k	e
ke	

k	i
ki	

k	o
ko	

k	u
ku	

Now say the sounds after me.

74   75

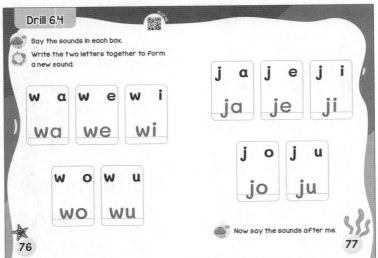

Drill 6.4

Say the sounds in each box.

Write the two letters together to form a new sound.

w	a
wa	

w	e
we	

w	i
wi	

w	o
wo	

w	u
wu	

j	a
ja	

j	e
je	

j	i
ji	

j	o
jo	

j	u
ju	

Now say the sounds after me.

76   77

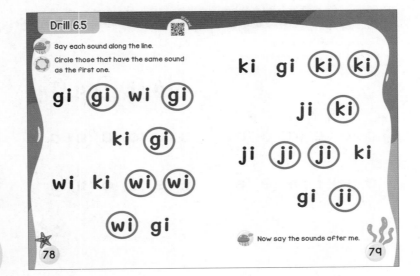

Drill 6.5

Say each sound along the line.

Circle those that have the same sound as the first one.

gi (gi) wi (gi)

ki (gi)

wi ki (wi) (wi)

(wi) gi

ki gi (ki) (ki)

ji (ki)

ji (ji) (ji) ki

gi (ji)

Now say the sounds after me.

78   79

156

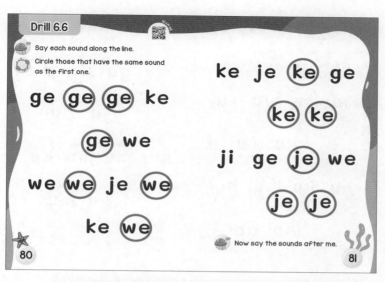

Drill 6.6

Say each sound along the line.

Circle those that have the same sound as the first one.

ge (ge) (ge) ke

(ge) we

we (we) je (we)

ke (we)

80

ke je (ke) ge

(ke) (ke)

ji ge (je) we

(je) (je)

Now say the sounds after me.

81

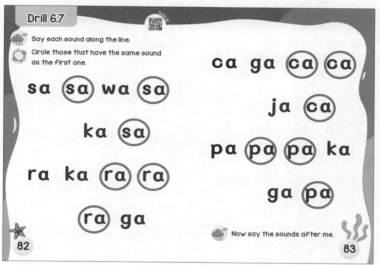

Drill 6.7

Say each sound along the line.

Circle those that have the same sound as the first one.

sa (sa) wa (sa)

ka (sa)

ra ka (ra) (ra)

(ra) ga

82

ca ga (ca) (ca)

ja (ca)

pa (pa) (pa) ka

ga (pa)

Now say the sounds after me.

83

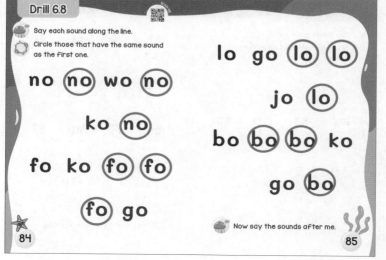

Drill 6.8

Say each sound along the line.

Circle those that have the same sound as the first one.

no (no) wo (no)

ko (no)

fo ko (fo) (fo)

(fo) go

84

lo go (lo) (lo)

jo (lo)

bo (bo) (bo) ko

go (bo)

Now say the sounds after me.

85

157

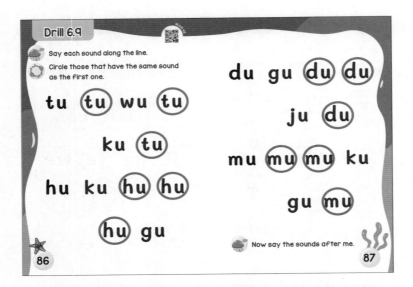

Drill 6.9

Say each sound along the line.

Circle those that have the same sound as the first one.

tu (tu) wu (tu)

ku (tu)

hu ku (hu) (hu)

(hu) gu

du gu (du) (du)

ju (du)

mu (mu) (mu) ku

gu (mu)

Now say the sounds after me.

86 87

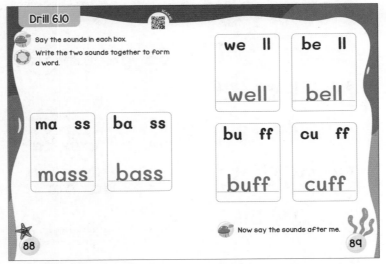

Drill 6.10

Say the sounds in each box.

Write the two sounds together to form a word.

ma ss	ba ss
mass	bass

we ll	be ll
well	bell

bu ff	cu ff
buff	cuff

Now say the sounds after me.

88 89

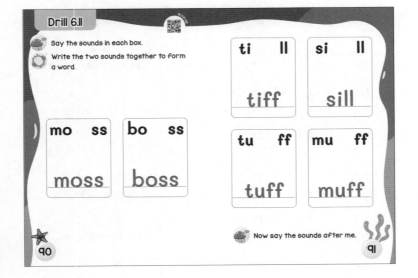

Drill 6.11

Say the sounds in each box.

Write the two sounds together to form a word.

mo ss	bo ss
moss	boss

ti ll	si ll
tiff	sill

tu ff	mu ff
tuff	muff

Now say the sounds after me.

90 91

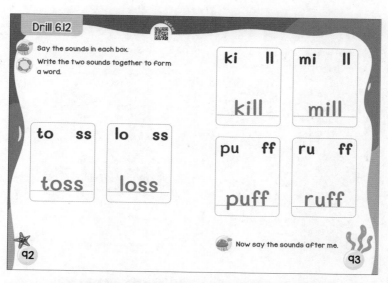

Drill 6.12

Say the sounds in each box.

Write the two sounds together to form a word.

ki	ll	mi	ll
kill		**mill**	

to	ss	lo	ss
toss		**loss**	

pu	ff	ru	ff
puff		**ruff**	

Now say the sounds after me.

92

93

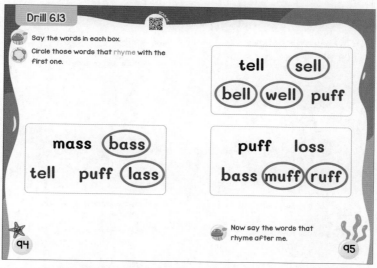

Drill 6.13

Say the words in each box.

Circle those words that rhyme with the first one.

tell (sell)
(bell) (well) puff

mass (bass)
tell puff (lass)

puff loss
bass (muff) (ruff)

Now say the words that rhyme after me.

94

95

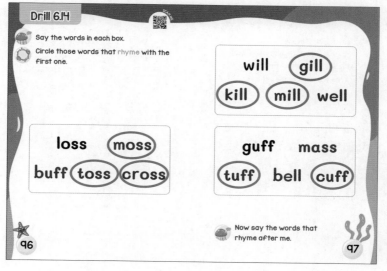

Drill 6.14

Say the words in each box.

Circle those words that rhyme with the first one.

will (gill)
(kill) (mill) well

loss (moss)
buff (toss) (cross)

guff mass
(tuff) bell (cuff)

Now say the words that rhyme after me.

96

97

159

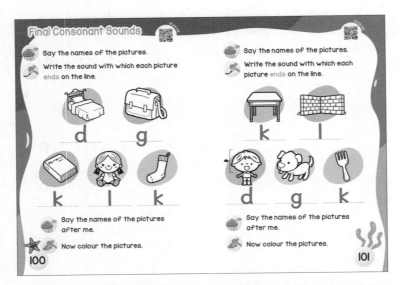

Final Consonant Sounds

Say the names of the pictures.

Write the sound with which each picture ends on the line.

d   g

k   l   k

Say the names of the pictures after me.

Now colour the pictures.

100

Say the names of the pictures.

Write the sound with which each picture ends on the line.

k   l

d   g   k

Say the names of the pictures after me.

Now colour the pictures.

101

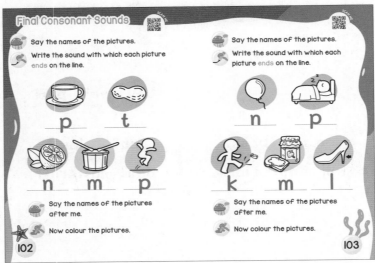

Final Consonant Sounds

Say the names of the pictures.

Write the sound with which each picture ends on the line.

p   t

n   m   p

Say the names of the pictures after me.

Now colour the pictures.

102

Say the names of the pictures.

Write the sound with which each picture ends on the line.

n   p

k   m   l

Say the names of the pictures after me.

Now colour the pictures.

103

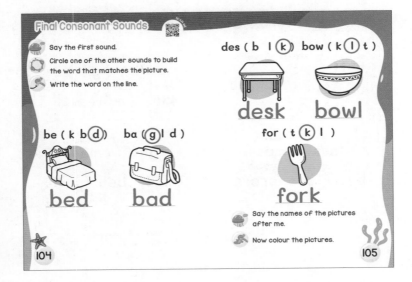

Final Consonant Sounds

Say the first sound.

Circle one of the other sounds to build the word that matches the picture.

Write the word on the line.

be (k b (d))   ba ((g) l d)

bed   bad

des (b l (k))   bow (k (l) t)

desk   bowl

for (t (k) l)

fork

Say the names of the pictures after me.

Now colour the pictures.

104   105

160

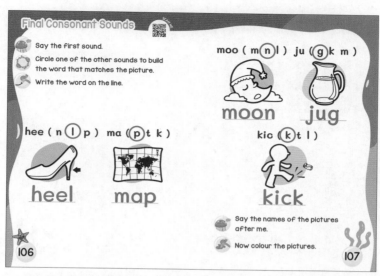

Final Consonant Sounds

Say the first sound.

Circle one of the other sounds to build the word that matches the picture.

Write the word on the line.

moo (m (n) l)   ju ((g) k m)

moon   **jug**

hee (n (l) p)   ma ((p) t k)

heel   **map**

kic ((k) t l)

kick

Say the names of the pictures after me.

Now colour the pictures.

106   107

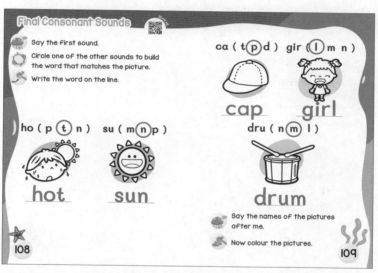

Final Consonant Sounds

Say the first sound.

Circle one of the other sounds to build the word that matches the picture.

Write the word on the line.

ca (t (p) d)   gir ((l) m n)

cap   **girl**

ho (p (t) n)   su (m (n) p)

hot   **sun**

dru (n (m) l)

drum

Say the names of the pictures after me.

Now colour the pictures.

108   109

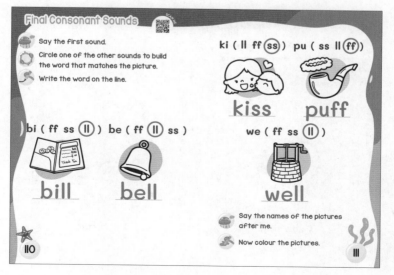

Final Consonant Sounds

Say the first sound.

Circle one of the other sounds to build the word that matches the picture.

Write the word on the line.

ki (ll ff (ss))   pu (ss ll (ff))

kiss   **puff**

bi (ff ss (ll))   be (ff (ll) ss)

bill   **bell**

we (ff ss (ll))

well

Say the names of the pictures after me.

Now colour the pictures.

110   111

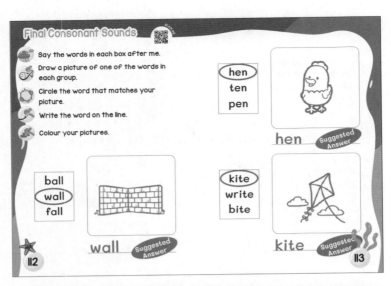

Final Consonant Sounds

- Say the words in each box after me.
- Draw a picture of one of the words in each group.
- Circle the word that matches your picture.
- Write the word on the line.
- Colour your pictures.

hen
ten
pen

hen   *Suggested Answer*

ball
wall
fall

wall   *Suggested Answer*

kite
write
bite

kite   *Suggested Answer*

112
113

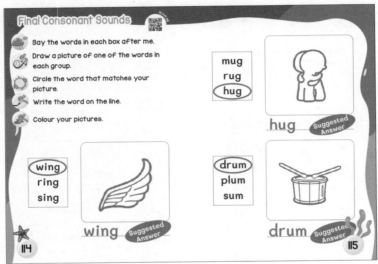

Final Consonant Sounds

- Say the words in each box after me.
- Draw a picture of one of the words in each group.
- Circle the word that matches your picture.
- Write the word on the line.
- Colour your pictures.

mug
rug
hug

hug   *Suggested Answer*

wing
ring
sing

wing   *Suggested Answer*

drum
plum
sum

drum   *Suggested Answer*

114
115

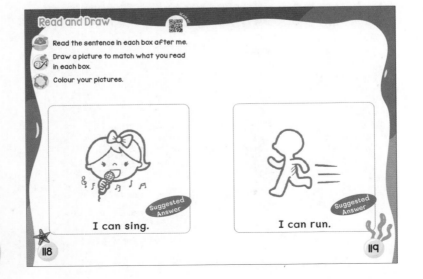

Read and Draw

- Read the sentence in each box after me.
- Draw a picture to match what you read in each box.
- Colour your pictures.

I can sing.   *Suggested Answer*

I can run.   *Suggested Answer*

118
119

Read and Draw

Read the sentence in each box after me.

Draw a picture to match what you read in each box.

Colour your pictures.

Suggested Answer

I kiss Mom.

Suggested Answer

I play with Dad.

120

121

Read and Draw

Read the words in each box after me.

Draw a picture to match what you read in each box.

Colour your pictures.

Suggested Answer

A man with a gun.

Suggested Answer

A doll in a bed.

122

123

Read and Draw

Read the words in each box after me.

Draw what the words tell you to do.

Colour your pictures.

Suggested Answer

Draw a hat on the girl.

Suggested Answer

Draw a bell on the dog.

124

125

Read the words in each box after me.

Draw what the words tell you to do.

Colour your pictures.

Suggested Answer

Draw six stars in the sky.

126

Suggested Answer

Draw eight eggs on the plate.

127

Read and Draw

Read the words in each box after me.

Draw what the words tell you to do.

Colour your pictures.

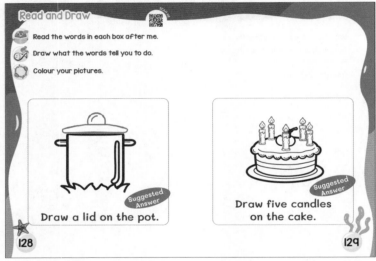

Suggested Answer

Draw a lid on the pot.

128

Suggested Answer

Draw five candles on the cake.

129

Say and Match

Say the words in the box after me.

Find the words that match each picture and write them on the line.

A lion   A snake

A hen   A monkey

A lion

A hen

A snake

A monkey

Say the words after me.

Now colour the pictures.

132

133

164

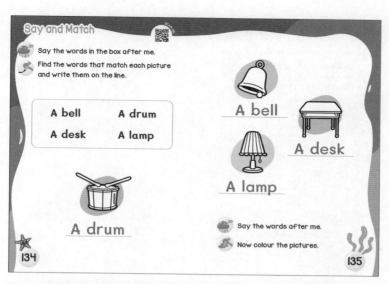

Say the words in the box after me.

Find the words that match each picture and write them on the line.

A bell   A drum

A desk   A lamp

A drum

A bell

A desk

A lamp

Say the words after me.

Now colour the pictures.

134

135

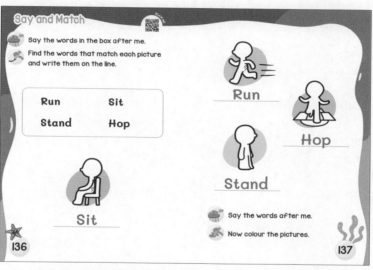

Say and Match

Say the words in the box after me.

Find the words that match each picture and write them on the line.

Run   Sit

Stand   Hop

Run

Hop

Stand

Sit

Say the words after me.

Now colour the pictures.

136

137

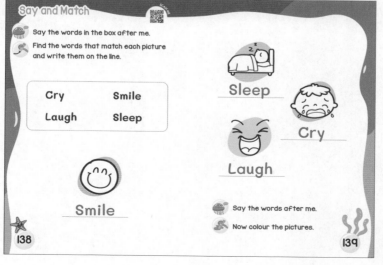

Say and Match

Say the words in the box after me.

Find the words that match each picture and write them on the line.

Cry   Smile

Laugh   Sleep

Sleep

Cry

Laugh

Smile

Say the words after me.

Now colour the pictures.

138

139

165

Tell a Story

- Read the sentence in each box after me.
- Draw a picture to match the sentence in each box.
- The pictures tell a story.
- Colour your pictures.

1

Suggested Answer

I eat the bread.

2

Suggested Answer

I drink the milk.

3

Suggested Answer

I go to school.